SAM RAZOR
PRIVATE INVESTIGATOR
his second case

THE BACKCOURT BLACK MAILER

Carlo Armenise

Author's Tranquility Press
ATLANTA, GEORGIA

Copyright © 2024 by Carlo Armenise

All rights reserved. No part of this publication may be reproduced, distributed or transmitted in any form or by any means, including photocopying, recording, or other electronic or mechanical methods, without the prior written permission of the publisher, except in the case of brief quotations embodied in critical reviews and certain other noncommercial uses permitted by copyright law. For permission requests, write to the publisher, addressed "Attention: Permissions Coordinator," at the address below.

Carlo Armenise / Author's Tranquility Press
3900 N Commerce Dr. Suite 300 #1255
Atlanta, GA 30344, USA
www.authorstranquilitypress.com

Ordering Information:
Quantity sales. Special discounts are available on quantity purchases by corporations, associations, and others. For details, contact the "Special Sales Department" at the address above.

Sam Razor: The Backcourt Blackmailer / Carlo Armenise
http://carloarmenise.com/

Paperback: 978-1-966088-06-6
eBook: 978-1-965463-79-6

Contents

Chapter One 1
Chapter Two 17
Chapter Three 25
Chapter Four 39
Chapter Five 51

Chapter One
THE PLAYOFFS

The most important things to the average guy are sex and sports. And having sex while watching sports is the ultimate. My sport of choice is basketball, and in L.A., where I live now, there are two professional basketball teams. One that's constantly great and the other that's continually rebuilding, in other words, sucks.

The Los Angeles Tigers are the reigning NBA Champs and sailed through the opening rounds of this year's playoffs. And while every bookie in town has them favored to repeat, the championship series won't be a gimme. It's against the New York Blazers, the team with the best record in the league and the team it took the Tigers seven games to beat the year before.

While even giving up your firstborn couldn't get you a ticket to the series, a client who runs a sports marketing company representing the Tigers hooked me up. I proved his wife was cheating and saved him a significant settlement in their divorce. To show his appreciation, he gave me courtside tickets to all the home playoff games and set me up on a date with his cheerleader girlfriend's sister.

While I have a hard-and-fast rule not to go on blind dates because, in the past, when I did, I usually prayed for blindness myself, but this time, I decided to take a chance. The cheerleader was so beautiful; how bad could the sister be? Well, as usual, I was wrong. The sister didn't look anything like the girlfriend. She was tall and skinny. Real skinny. But considering I'd be sitting courtside and getting up close and personal with movie stars and my favorite basketball team, I decided to go on the date and make the best of it.

We get to the arena an hour before the game to watch the players warm up and are escorted to our court-side seats. I can't tell you how excited I am. Sitting just feet away from the players I watch on T.V. made me think of times when I watched Tiger games with my dad and younger brother, Marco. My dad was a big-time Tigers fan and would record and repeatedly watch every one of their games, win or lose. So, to spend time with him, Marco and I started rooting for the Tigers, too, and would watch the games and place bets. Marco and my dad always took the Tigers, and I always took the opposing team for fun. While we never bet more than a dollar, we got so competitive you would have thought we bet two dollars.

I remember one game when the Tigers were up by four points with only thirty seconds left. The Tigers had the ball, but instead of holding onto it and playing it safe, they tried some idiot play, lost it, and got beat. My dad got so mad that he started cussing, threw his beer can at the television, and stormed out of the room, refusing to pay me my dollar. He said he wasn't paying because the refs cost him the game. Bad refereeing was his go-to excuse anytime the Tigers lost, even if they lost by fifty points. But my brother and I didn't care; spending time with him was nice, regardless of how crazy he got. When he passed away, Marco and I stopped watching Tiger games together; it just wasn't the same. But now, every time I see a beer can on TV or a ref makes a call I don't like during a game, I think of my dad and smile. I know he died on purpose to keep from paying me my dollar. I miss you, Dad.

A few minutes after we got in our seats, Peter, the client who set me up with the tickets and date, walked up.

"Sam, I need to talk to you."

"And I need to talk to you," I say sarcastically, indicating my date.

"Phil Redman wants to see you."

"Phil Redman, the owner of the Tigers?"

"The same."

"Why does he want to see me?"

"He didn't tell me, but I wouldn't keep him waiting if I were you. Come on; I'll take you up to his private box."

"Lead on," I say as I excuse myself from my date and follow him.

"I'm sorry about your date, Sam. I took her sister's word when she said she was a real beauty."

"Well, she was right about the real part. Don't worry, she's nice, and the seats are amazing."

"Good."

On the way up to the private boxes at the top of the arena. I try to figure out why Phil Redman would want to see me. Not only is he one of the most powerful men in the world, with more money than God, which is a little less than Bill Gates, but he also has a reputation for being impulsive and once lost a million dollars in a game of one card War. I dream about having his kind of money and going to exotic places with the wealthy in-crowd. Don't get me wrong, I'm grateful for my life, but I'd be even more thankful, boarding on ecstatic, if I had his dough.

When Peter and I got to Redman's suite, at least fifteen mean-looking security guards checked our identification and frisked us. I remember thinking Redman either had a lot of enemies or a lot of people he didn't want to be his friend. Anyway, after the security goons touch and squeeze every inch of our bodies, a few places I wanted them to spend more time on, they take my gun, open the door, and let us in.

The suite is directly over the basketball court and is bigger than my condo. There are bars and buffet tables with booze and food in every corner of the room, and at least a hundred people dancing and drinking. And I'm not talking about ugly people, either. The least attractive woman in the room makes Pamela Anderson look like a truck driver, and the men are so pretty they make you think about turning gay. And while I've got nothing against gay guys, they make me uncomfortable. They're always well-groomed and well-dressed; they make me feel like a slob. I know about this stuff because my cousin Vinny is gay and dresses so well that he makes the rest of the family look like vagrants. He's been that way since kindergarten when his mother got him his first pair of Gucci loafers and Prada pants. He immediately started criticizing the other kindergarteners for how they dressed. Don't worry; the other kids got even. They peed in his chocolate milk and put peanut butter in his loafers.

After we walked into the suite, another bigger, meaner-looking security guard approached me.

"You Sam Razor?"

"That's right."

"Mr. Redman's waiting for you. Follow me."

I follow him to an interior office in the back of the suite, and he opens the door.

"Sam Razor, sir."

I enter the office and find Phil Redman talking on the phone behind a big, glass-top desk. He looks fifty-something, has salt and pepper hair, and is trim and in good shape. And while he isn't what I would call classically good-looking, considering how rich he is, who needs the classics? The office is enormous, with photos of Redman and various movie stars and politicians covering the walls. Behind Redman's desk is a trophy case stuffed with trophies, including the previous year's championship trophy. It's enormous and made of gold. It reminded me of the trophy I got for winning the L.A. Private Investigator Bowling Palooza, except that my trophy was tiny and made of plastic.

Redman motioned for me to sit, finished his call, walked over, and shook my hand.

"Sam, I'm Phil Redman."

"It's a pleasure meeting you, Mr. Redman."

"Call me Phil. Can I get you a drink?"

"Scotch and water would be great, Phil."

"Peter tells me you're good at what you do," he says as he walks to a bar and makes the drinks.

"I try."

"How long have you been a private investigator, Sam?" he asks as he hands me my drink and sits back at his desk.

"Fifteen years. I started working with my dad and took over his agency when he passed away."

"I lost my dad, too. You have my condolences."

"Thank you. And the same to you."

"What made you follow in your dad's footsteps, Sam?"

"Investigating runs in my family. Besides my dad, my grandfather and my great-grandfather were both private investigators. And my great-great-grandfather was cheating on his wife and got caught by a private investigator," I say jokingly.

Redman doesn't crack a smile, so I decide he either doesn't have a sense of humor or his great-great-grandfather did get caught cheating by a private investigator.

"How's the investigation business going, Sam?"

"Good. In L.A., there's always somebody cheating and somebody else that pays me to catch them."

"Handled anything other than divorces?"

"Yeah, a few months ago, when I was living in Las Vegas, I was involved with a kidnapping."

"That's right, it involved two wealthy sisters."

"Yeah, one of the sisters staged her kidnapping to swindle money from the other sister to pay a gambling debt."

"Bizarre. And didn't I read that somebody got killed?"

"One guy and almost two, if you count me."

He stops talking and stares at me. I know he's rich and powerful, but something about his stare feels slimy. But since it's rich and powerful slime, I'm okay with it.

"Sam, I assume you've heard of Rickie Wagner?"

Was he kidding? Everyone who follows sports knows Rickie Wagner. He's the star point guard for the Tigers, averaging a billion points a game, and easily the best player in the NBA. He was recruited out of high school and became the most popular player in the history of the NBA. Kids didn't just want to be like Rickie; they had plastic surgery to look like him. And even though the Tigers signed him to the richest contract in NBA history, he became a free agent after the playoffs and threatened to leave the team if his new contract demands weren't met.

"Is that a trick question?"

"Yeah, well, he could be in trouble," Redman says.

"What did he do, get a parking ticket?" I say sarcastically.

Since starting in the league, Rickie has been a model player and has never been involved in scandal or adversity. Everything about him is so clean; it's hard to imagine him ever needing to shower.

"It's more serious than that," Redman says as he opens a desk drawer, takes out an envelope, and hands it to me.

"Open it."

I opened the envelope and found a typed note addressed to Redman. It was from a blackmailer claiming irrefutable evidence that Rickie was addicted to heroin, owes millions to the Mexican cartel, and throws games to pay them back. And to keep from going public with the accusation, the blackmailer wanted seventy-five million dollars in one week.

"This is a serious accusation."

"Yes, it is."

"When did you get this?"

"Early this morning. I found it under my door."

"Why did the blackmailer send it to you and not Rickie?"

"Because they know I have the money and stand to lose a fuck of a lot more than seventy-five million if Rickie gets suspended by the league while they investigate the accusation, and we lose the series."

"What does Rickie say about it?"

"He doesn't know. I don't want to distract him. Besides, I know it's not true."

"What makes you so sure?"

"Because Rickie is a well-respected young man with a ton of integrity and moral character. He grew up in a religious home and was raised by a loving and tough-minded mother whom I've met several times. If Rickie did anything to tarnish his pristine persona and defame the Lord and his family, she'd cut his balls off. Besides, Rickie lives for basketball and wouldn't do anything to risk his career. So no, Rickie's not on drugs. I think somebody in my organization is trying to blackmail me."

"Why would they do that?"

I can see how he shifts in his chair and looks around the room; the question makes him uncomfortable.

"You want another drink?" He asks as he walks back to the bar.

"No thanks, I've got someone waiting for me," I reply, but then I remember my date and think about asking for a bottle to go.

"People in my organization don't like how I run things," he says as he walks over to the trophy case and looks at the championship trophy.

"But if you're sure the accusation's not true, why not just ignore it?"

"Because if I ignore it, and the blackmailer does go public, even if it's not true, the media circus and public insinuations will scar Rickie for the rest of his career. And considering we've lost every game without him being a hundred percent, we'll lose the championship and the billions of dollars of future ticket sales and television revenue that goes with it."

"Then it sounds like you're going to pay."

"No, I'm not. That's why I wanted to see you."

"Listen, I'd like to help, but I never carry more than seventy-four million on me," I say jokingly.

Not cracking a smile, he walked over to me and looked me in the eye.

"I want you to find out who the blackmailer is and prove the allegation is bullshit before the end of the week," he says seriously.

"What if I can't find out by then? Or what if the blackmailer isn't part of your organization?"

"If you're half as good as Peter says, I have faith you'll get it done."

He was right; I am half as good as Peter says I am. But it's still not much time.

"But why hire me? With your money, you could resurrect Sherlock Holmes."

"Not up to the job, Sam?"

"I didn't say that. I'm just curious."

"I picked you for two reasons. First, I trust Peter's judgment, and second, I want this investigation to be low profile. If I hire a famous detective, it will get too much attention. So, do you want the case or not?"

Was he kidding? I couldn't tell him, but I would do anything short of giving him a blowjob to get this job. Okay, so I would consider giving him a quick blowjob.

"Yes."

"Great. Now, what about your fee?"

"Well, my standard fee is a thousand dollars a day plus expenses, but considering my limited time, I'm thinking three thousand dollars a day."

I had just finished an online negotiation course and learned to start high and come down if needed. And considering how rich this guy was and that I could save him seventy-five million dollars, I didn't think I'd have to come down too far.

"I'll tell you what," he said, returning to his desk. "Considering how important it is that you find the blackmailer, I'll pay you ten thousand a day whether or not you find out who it is, and if you do find out who it is and stop it, I'll throw in a hundred-thousand-dollar bonus."

I had just taken a drink of scotch, and when I heard a hundred thousand, I choked and spit my drink out.

"Sorry," I said as I wiped off my shirt. "I always react like that when I hear the words " hundred and thousand " in the same sentence."

"So, it sounds like we've got a deal," he said, shaking my hand."

"When should I start?"

"First thing tomorrow morning. After every game, we have a post-game meeting, and at that meeting, I'll introduce you as our new Security Director. That will make it easy to investigate and ask questions without raising suspicion. And since I had a feeling we'd come to terms, I prepared background information on all the members of my management team," he says and hands me a manila envelope. "That way, you can get familiar with them before the meeting."

This guy is a smooth operator, and I like his hundred-grand operating style. "Great," I say as I stand up. "Then I'll see you in the morning. I've got to get back to my date."

"Why don't you bring her here and watch the game from the suite?"

Normally, I would have jumped at the chance to mix and mingle with Redman and his bevy of beauties, but to save a little of what's left of my already suspect reputation with the ladies, I decided it would be better if my date and I stayed where we were.

"Thanks for the offer, but it's our first date, and I want to keep it more intimate. If you know what I mean?"

"Hoping to get lucky, huh?"

"Yeah, lucky," I say, forcing a smile.

"Then I'll see you in the morning. Enjoy the game."

"I will, but only if the Tigers win."

The Tigers did win, and the game was great. Rickie scored thirty-eight points and the game-winning basket. If he was shaving points, he could use a better razor. As I watch the arena crowd give the team a standing ovation as they walk off the court after the game and see how loved Rickie is, I decide Redman's right; the drug allegation has to be bullshit.

After the game, as my date and I returned to my car, all I could think about was how stupid I was to accept this case. While the ten grand a day and hundred thousand bonus sounded good, if I couldn't deliver and Redman lost Rickie or millions of dollars, I know he isn't the type of guy who takes failure well and is good at revenge. After I dropped my date off at her apartment, I headed home to review the information Redman gave me. She begged me to spend the night, but I told her I never had sex on the first date. Okay, I'm lying. Considering I hadn't been laid in a while, I thought about staying and jumping her bones. But since she was nothing but bones, I passed and returned to my apartment and spent the rest of the night reading about Redman's illustrious cast of characters. Since they were all well-known in L.A., I knew quite a bit about them from local news.

First on the Redman's list was Al Johnson, the Tiger's Hall of Fame white head coach. Johnson started his coaching career as an assistant with the Dallas Jets and, in just two years, was offered the head coaching job for the New Jersey Jammers. After taking the Jammers to ten playoffs and two championships, Redman offered him colossal money to join the Tigers and bring a title to L.A., and that's what he did. In his first year with the Tigers, Johnson took the team to the division championship and increased the wealth of the franchise by two hundred percent. But while his results on the court were impressive, he had his share of controversy off the court. He claimed he was broke because of costly divorces and bad investments. And even though he was already the league's highest-paid head coach, he threatened to quit if Redman didn't give him more money. And if that didn't rock the proverbial boat enough, Johnson also wanted Redman to trade Rickie. He said it was because Rickie's ego caused trouble with the other players. The truth was, Johnson didn't like Rickie because he was too popular with the fans and knew Redman would give him anything he wanted to stay with the team, even if that meant losing Johnson. While, on the surface, it seems the head coach has a double motive for blackmail, money, and hatred, the question is, would a Hall of Famer be stupid enough to go that far?

Next on the list is Redman's younger brother, Jerry. Jerry Redman had been a star player with the Tigers for twelve years until he tore a few things in his knee and had to stop playing. But when he did, he made it known in the press that he wanted to be a coach. So, when his brother bought the Tigers, Jerry asked him for a coaching job, and Phil made him an assistant coach with the promise that he would get the top job after getting coaching experience. Six years later, Jerry felt he had paid his dues as an assistant and was ready to move up. So, when Redman fired the head coach before Johnson, Jerry reminded his brother, in the press again, of his promise to make him the head Honcho. But, unknown to Jerry, Redman had already hired Johnson and turned his brother down. Redman was quoted in the paper saying his brother was too valuable as an assistant. But the truth was Redman needed a head coach with a championship pedigree, and Jerry didn't have it. While Phil agreed to keep Jerry on with the organization, he couldn't risk creating animosity with Johnson keeping him on as an assistant, so instead, he offered Jerry the back-office General Manager's job.

While Jerry knew his brother was doing it to keep him from causing trouble, it came with a significant salary increase and let him be close to the action, so he agreed. Four years later, in his new role, Jerry pulled off the deal of the century and signed Rickie. And while Jerry stayed on with the organization and didn't make a big deal about his brother screwing him over for the coaching job, everyone knew it damaged their relationship. My question was, was the relationship just damaged or completely broken? And would Jerry stoop to blackmailing his brother and sacrifice Rickie to do it?

Redman's current wife, Lisa, was next on the list. Lisa was a beautiful, black former Tiger's cheerleader and Playboy playmate—specifically, Miss October. Lisa wasn't just attractive; she was also brilliant. She got her hooks into Redman at a party at the Playboy mansion, and they were married a week later. Since I'm currently divorced, I'm not big on marriage, let alone after only a week, but in Lisa's case, a week was six days too long. But since Lisa is thirty-five years younger than Redman and a past playboy playmate, to the press, she's nothing more than a gold digger with big boobs.

Carlo Armenise

I don't find anything wrong with being a gold-digger; I would love to find an older woman with a ton of money to take care of me. Unfortunately, all the women I meet who fit that profile are so old they can't remember they have money. But honestly, even that kind of relationship wouldn't work for me. I have what my shrink calls 'commitment phobia.' It started when I was in high school. I was short and fat, and while the other guys were chasing and getting chased by girls, I was pursuing my right hand and being turned down. Besides being fat, I also had terrible acne and crooked teeth; it was the perfect storm of ugly. My acne was so bad that the science teacher used my face as a simulated moon surface, and my teeth were so crooked my braces needed braces.

But a few years later, after losing weight, getting my teeth fixed, and getting my acne cleaned up, I met my soul mate, Maryann, and we married. For six months until she started fooling around with the Amazon delivery driver and divorced me. Now I know why she got so many packages. She said she divorced me because she realized I wasn't her type. I knew that was a bull-shit excuse because I didn't know how to type. So, since then, I've been alone, except for Frank, the chihuahua she left, and looking for that next special someone and getting intimate with Lisa Redman's past Playboy photoshoots.

After they married, Redman brought Lisa into the basketball business and put her in charge of the cheerleading squad. It's a nothing position, but it gives her a reason to come to the office, to be with Redman. While on the surface, the relationship between Redman and Lisa looks like a match made in 'gold digger' heaven, I remembered reading that before the wedding, Redman forced Lisa to sign a prenup that entitled her to only a million dollars if, for any reason, the marriage didn't last. And even though she agreed, according to the tabloids, she was pissed because, in L.A., minimum wage is more than that. So yeah, Lisa could have a greedy motive to blackmail Redman, but considering the lifestyle she'd be losing if it didn't work, would she risk it?

The other thing the press said about Lisa is that she's a real bitch, and doesn't get along with anyone in the organization, especially Redman's daughter Christina. Christina is Redman's only child and the company president, running all her father's business interests, including the Tigers.

Christina is beautiful and holds an MBA from Harvard. She came to work for her father after spending several successful years on Wall Street as an executive at a top investment firm. Rumor has it she wanted to prove she could make it on her own before agreeing to come to work with Daddy. Another story about Christina is that she's a hard ass that takes no prisoners. And while she loves to piss her father off in the press by criticizing his marriage to Lisa, on the surface, it doesn't look like she has a motive for blackmail. But then again, as my dad, God rest his soul, always said, the surface is only skin deep.

And then there's Redman himself. And even though he didn't give me any personal background information, I knew all about him from his press coverage. Besides being an eccentric billionaire, he's ruthless with his business interests, especially the Tigers. As I mentioned before, Rickie was becoming a free agent after the playoffs unless he and Redman could agree on the terms of a new contract. According to Rickie's agent, that contract needed to include an ownership stake in the team. And while I don't know Redman at all, given his reputation, I know he wasn't the type to give anything to anybody that wasn't in his best interest. So even though Rickie seemed to have Redman by his rich, big, slimy balls, don't forget, slime is slippery and hard to hold onto.

After spending all night analyzing Redman's team and using my crack investigator instincts, I came to one unmistakable conclusion on the way to the arena: I had no fucking idea who the blackmailer was. I got to the arena an hour before the meeting and parked near the employee entrance to watch the others arrive. In my line of work, you spend a lot of time in your car spying on people to catch them cheating, so you learn how to see without being seen.

Take my friend Peter's divorce case, for example. Before he and his wife married, they signed a prenup that said if either of them were unfaithful during the marriage, the guilty party would give up all rights to whatever their estate was worth at the time of the divorce. In the beginning, considering they were young and didn't have shit, the agreement didn't mean much. But fifteen years into the marriage, with them worth millions, the wife decided they had irreconcilable differences and wanted a divorce and her half of the estate.

That's when Peter came to me, suspecting her irreconcilable differences involved having an affair with his business partner. And after only a week of 'car-veillance', I found out he was right. His wife and business partner were having an affair, but not with one another. His partner was having an affair with his trainer, his 'male' personal trainer, and his wife was screwing a young, good-looking grocery store delivery boy. A couple of times a week, she would call the store and order a couple of gallons of milk, two loaves of bread, and a big sausage; it gave a whole new meaning to the term 'home delivery.' And since the original prenup was still in effect, and I proved she was having an affair, the sausage cost Peter's wife a cool five million. It just goes to show how inflation has affected meat prices.

The following day, after I walked Frank, I left for the arena. I never knew why my ex-wife named him Frank. But I figured out it was because he would bark and get excited whenever he saw an Amazon truck. And since I didn't want to confuse him and change his name to something more dog-like, like Fido or Mutt, I just left his name, Frank. A few minutes after I get to the arena and park so I can see the arena entrance, a brand-new big-ass Mercedes SUV with a license plate reading 'Main Man' pulls in and parks next to me, and Al Johnson gets out. He looked nine feet tall, was in great shape, and wore an expensive black designer sweatsuit with his name embossed in big gold letters on the back of the jacket. When I saw his coat, it reminded me of my dad's brother, Uncle Tony. He considered himself the best basketball player in our family and always wore a black sweatsuit with his name written on the back of the jacket in magic marker. While he was right, he was the best basketball player in the family; he was only five feet tall, fat, slow, and couldn't jump, evidenced by the fact we measured his vertical leap with a paperclip. So being the best player in our family didn't mean much. But we let him have his delusions since he brought the beer to all the family functions.

As Johnson walks toward the arena, he takes out his cell phone and makes a call.

"Yeah, it's me. No, that's not going to work. I'll handle it myself. Goodbye," he says, then hangs up the call and walks into the arena.

It was apparent Al had something to handle, but was it blackmail? A few minutes later, another black Mercedes sports car pulled into the lot, parked in a reserved space near the entrance, and Lisa Redman got out, also talking on her cell phone. She was even more gorgeous in person than in her pictures. She has shoulder-length blonde hair, a perfect petite little body, and big boobs, and is wearing tight-fitting, low-riding jeans and a blouse that is so low cut and revealing it's almost invisible. And now that I see her, I'm sure Redman is giving her anything she wants, despite the prenup. Because she's laughing while talking, and Johnson wasn't, I surmise she isn't talking to Johnson. As she walks toward the arena, I can't resist sticking my head out the driver's side window to get a better look at her ass.

As I'm dangling out my window, a Lincoln Navigator, playing loud rap music, pulls in and parks in another reserved space in front of my car, and Jerry Redman gets out, also talking on his cell phone. He's taller than Johnson, has long black scraggly hair, a full beard, and is dressed in jeans and a Tiger's sweatshirt. As he walked past my car, I quickly pulled myself back inside, ducked down, and moved close to the window to hear his conversation.

"Don't worry. Everything's going to work out just like we planned. I got to go. I'll call you after the meeting," Jerry says, then hangs up the call, puts the phone in his pocket, and walks into the arena.

Even though I don't know who he's talking to, I can tell he's planning something and has a partner, but is it Johnson?"

Since it's almost nine and I don't want to be late for the meeting, I leave my car and walk toward the arena. At that moment, a security van with its flashing lights pulls up and stops beside me.

"Stop right there," says an older, well-muscled security guard as he jumps out of the van and runs over to me, "Who are you? And what are you doing here?"

"My name's Sam Razor. I'm here to see Mr. Redman."

"Is that right? Well, I got a report that a pervert was in the parking lot spying on women."

"Do I look like a pervert?" I ask, realizing Lisa Redman must have caught me investigating her ass and reported me. "I told you; Phil Redman is expecting me. Call his office and check."

"I'll do that. Wait here," the guard says as he takes his walkie-talkie and turns his back to me.

While the guard checks my story, I keep thinking that if Lisa did see me, she'd recognize me as the pervert when we meet. What excuse will I give? And even worse, if she tells her husband what happened, I'll get fired even before I start and lose out on the hundred grand bonus. As I'm about to return to my car and leave to save myself from embarrassment, the guard finishes his call and turns back to me.

"You can go right in, Mr. Razor. Mr. Redman is expecting you. And I'm sorry if I was out of line. It must have been someone else."

"No problem, you were just doing your job."

"Thank you, sir," he says as he returns to his van and drives away.

Still stressed that Lisa would recognize me and tell her husband, I remembered something my dad had said to me when I'd stress out about something that hadn't happened yet.

"Remember, Sam; there's enough actual bad shit that happens in life without worrying about shit that may never happen."

As usual, Dad was right. So, I decided if Lisa did recognize me as the pervert, seeing her ass was worth it, and I smiled and walked into the arena.

Chapter Two
THE PLAYERS

Because the security guard stopped me, I was a few minutes late to the meeting and expected it to be underway. But Redman was the only one there when I entered the conference room.

"Good to see you, Sam. How are you?" he asks as he walks over and shakes my hand.

"Good. Sorry, I'm late. Is the meeting over?"

"No, it hasn't started yet. Nobody around here is ever on time for meetings. Help yourself to some breakfast," he says, walking over to a table covered with breakfast foods and coffee, pouring himself a cup, and then sitting at a conference table. "How'd you like the game?"

"It was great," I reply as I pour myself a cup of coffee and join him at the table. "I can see what you mean about Rickie. He's a class act and a fan favorite, not your typical drug addict."

"Yeah. Did you get a chance to review the background information I gave you?"

"Yes."

"Have any thoughts?"

"Not yet, but I'm eager to meet them all in person."

"Don't forget, I'll introduce you as our replacement director of security."

"What happened to your last security director?"

"I had to fire him. He was making Lisa uncomfortable. She said he was a pervert and wouldn't stop staring at her tits when he talked to her. I didn't see the problem. I mean, she's already shown a fuck of a lot more than her tits in Playboy, right? But now that she's my wife, she wants people to appreciate her for more than her body."

The second I heard Lisa call the other guy a pervert, I knew for sure she was the one who called security. As I stressed out again, the conference room door opened, and Lisa walked in.

"Don't tell me I'm the first one to the fucking meeting again," she says as she walks over and kisses Redman.

"Lisa, I want you to meet Sam Razor, our new head of security. Sam, this is my wife, Lisa."

"It's nice to meet you, Mrs. Redman," I say as I stand up and shake her hand.

"You, too," she says and stares at my face. "Have we met before? You look familiar."

"No, but I've seen you in pictures," I say, staring at her eyes.

"Are you talking about those stupid ass Playboy photoshoots?" she says disgustedly.

"Yes, but I have to say your pictures don't do justice to your eyes. They're stunning."

When I recognize something about her besides her body, she forgets her suspicions and smiles.

"Thank you, Sam, that's so sweet. I think my eyes are my best feature. That and my tits," she says, laughing. "Well, welcome aboard, and if there's anything I can do to help you, just let me know."

"I will, thank you," I say with a sigh of relief.

"You boys will have to excuse me; I have to take a piss. I mean, use the little girls' room," she smiles. "I'll be right back," she says, leaving the conference room.

"Nice work, Sam," Redman says. "I think you won her over."

"Thanks, but her eyes are beautiful."

"Sure, and so is the rest of her. Listen, how will we interact as your investigation progresses?"

"After I've had a chance to talk to everybody, I'll come and tell you if I find out anything."

"Good. And I'm the only one. Nobody else can know."

At that moment, an older woman walks into the conference room.

"Mr. Redman, Mr. Dunlap is on the phone."

"Thank you, Eloise. Sam, I'll be back in a minute."

After Redman and Eloise walked out, I looked around the conference room. The walls are lined with Tiger's game photos, including one of Rickie throwing down a monster dunk, and as I walk over to take a closer look, Rickie walks into the room.

"You like that shot?" he asks as he approaches me.

Rickie is an impressive physical specimen. He's six-ten, covered in muscle, and has movie-star looks.

"Are you kidding?" I say, "That was a classic. The sportswriters called it 'the dunk felt round the world.' It was two years ago against Atlanta, and if I remember right, you scored a career-high fifty-two points in that game."

"Impressive," Rickie says, smiling. "But it was fifty-three points."

"I stand corrected. I'm Sam Razor, the new head of security," I say, shaking his hand.

"I remember seeing you at last night's game," he said, returning my handshake. "You were sitting courtside next to that real skinny girl."

"Yeah, that was me," I reply sheepishly. "You played a hell of a game."

"Thanks. So, you're replacing Tom."

"Tom?" I ask.

"The old head of security. I'm glad he's gone. He wasn't very good."

"Why do you say that?"

"Because there's a lot of weird shit going on in this place, and he didn't do anything to stop it."

As I started to ask him more about the 'weird shit,' the conference door opened again, and Jerry Redman, Christina Redman, and Al Johnson all walked in. Al and Rickie exchanged dirty looks as Al walked past us, and Rickie looked back at me.

"It was nice meeting you, Sam. I've got to get back to the gym, but tell Phil I'll come and see him later. And good luck."

"Thanks."

As Rickie walks out of the room, he passes Christina Redman.

"You played a great game last night, Rickie," Christina says.

"Thanks, Chris."

"Yeah," Jerry says. "Three more like that, and the championship is in the bag."

"What about you, Coach?" Rickie asks Al. "Do you think I played a great game?" he says sarcastically.

Johnson doesn't respond and walks to the other side of the room. Rickie laughs and walks out of the conference room. While it was apparent that Al and Rickie don't like one another, I wonder if it has anything to do with the things Rickie mentioned. As everyone took seats at the conference table, Christina Redman approached me. She's stunning. Tall and thin with long, jet-black hair and piercing blue eyes. And even though she makes every attempt to hide her feminine assets under a costly and very conservative business suit, a couple of things sticking out on her chest tell me she's all woman.

"I'm Christina Redman," she says, holding her hand to shake.

"Nice meeting you, Christina," I reply, shaking her hand. "I'm …"

"Sam Razor. My father told me all about you."

"He did?" I reply.

"Yes, he said he hired you to replace Tom."

"Right."

"Come sit next to me," she says and sits at the conference table.

As I sat down next to Christina, Redman and Lisa walked back into the room and took seats next to one another at one end of the table.

"It looks like we're all here, finally, so let's get started," Redman says as he takes a paper pad with notes.

Before he starts to talk, I survey the table to see if I can pick up any subtle body language that gives me a clue about the kidnapper's identity. Jerry is sitting on the other side of Christina but doesn't look at his brother. It was apparent they still had their issues. While Lisa and Christina looked at one another, all they did was scowl. And Al, sitting at the other side of the table by himself, glares at everybody. The hate in the room is so strong I can smell it. And thanks to my nasty divorce, I'm an expert on the smell of hatred. It smells like anger with a dash of disgust.

As Redman started the meeting, I paid particular attention to Jerry. If the person he talked to on the phone about his plan is one of the other people at the table, I'm confident they will either make eye contact or do something that will indicate who it is.

"Our first order of business is for me to introduce our new security director, Sam Razor," Redman says. "Sam is replacing Tom and will report to me and be in Tom's old office. Sam comes to us with years of experience in security and private investigation, so I know he'll immediately make a positive impact. Right, Sam?" he says and looks at me.

As everyone at the table turns and looks at me, expecting me to talk, I get nervous. I have a phobia regarding public speaking. I remember almost pissing my pants when my dad would make me say grace in front of a table full of hungry relatives on Thanksgiving. And now, to speak to a group of rich, powerful, famous people expecting me to say something intelligent makes my knees weaken, and I start to sweat. At that moment, I remember a little trick my high school speech teacher, Miss Pennywhistle, taught me to calm my nerves. She said whenever I had to talk to a group of strangers and got nervous, I should imagine them all naked; that way, they'd be less intimidating. So, that's what I did. I pictured everyone at the table in their birthday suits, and it worked like a charm, and I relaxed. With everyone except Lisa Redman and Christina, imagining them naked makes me horny.

"I want to say how fortunate I am to be a part of such an incredible sports organization. The Tigers have always been my family's favorite professional basketball team. And getting the opportunity to work with such a revered group of professionals is a great honor. I plan to meet with you all at some point today to understand where each of you thinks the security department needs to improve. And if there are any immediate issues I need to look into right away, please let me know. Thank you."

Redman looked at me as I finished talking and put everybody but Lisa's clothes back on.

"Thank you, Sam. Any questions for Sam?" he asks.

Nobody says anything. They ignore me and stay focused on their obvious disgust for one another.

"Fine," Redman says. "I know I can count on everyone to cooperate with Sam, just like you did with Tom. Now, let's move on and talk about last night's game."

Besides Redman and Johnson, nobody else says much during the rest of the meeting, and Jerry doesn't do anything to indicate that his phone mate is in the room. After the meeting was over and everybody had left, Redman approached me.

"So, now that you've met them all, what's your impression?"

"Well, for one thing, it's clear they don't like one another very much."

"And me most of all," he says. "And that's why I know one of them is behind the blackmail."

"But not liking you, in and of itself, isn't usually a motive for a seventy-five-million-dollar blackmail plot."

"I know, but trust me, one of them is behind it."

While I hear what he says, my instincts tell me Redman knows more about who the blackmailer is than he's letting on. Besides his management team, according to the press, Redman is also hated by several people outside his organization. The Mayor of Los Angeles hates him for lobbying to kick him out of office. The NBA Commissioner hates him for ignoring free agency rules, and the President of the Players Association hates him for fighting against the Association's attempts to get better league retirement benefits.

"Who do you think it is?" I ask.

"I don't know," he says. "It could be any one of them except for my daughter. We have our issues, but Christina wouldn't do anything to hurt me or Rickie."

"What about the others?"

"Well, my brother and I haven't been close for a long time. I think he's weak, and he thinks I'm a greedy asshole, and we're both right. And when I didn't give him the Tiger's head coaching job, it got worse."

It's funny, Redman's relationship with his brother was just like mine and my brother's, minus their shit load of money. My brother Marco and I spent our entire childhood fighting with one another, and he'd always use physical force to get his way because he was bigger. In fact, by the time I was ten, he had given me so many atomic wedgies that I had to have my underwear surgically removed from my asshole. But as we got older and matured emotionally and I got bigger, we sorted out our differences and started to get along. But just in case, I kept wearing tear-away underwear.

"Why didn't you give your brother the job?" I asked.

"He wasn't qualified. I needed a coach with championship experience. Besides, my brother was just a mediocre player, not head coach material."

"And you think he could still want revenge?"

"Oh, he wants it, but he's got it too good to risk it. I pay him a fuck load of money, plus all kinds of other perks. And besides, he's not smart enough to pull it off blackmail by himself."

"What about Johnson? He hates Rickie, and you know he wants more money."

"Yeah, but he's got it good with the Tigers. He's the highest-paid coach in the NBA and knows no other team will pay him that much."

"But do you think he'd resort to blackmail?"

"That's what you're going to find out, right?" he says with a definite, serious tone.

"Right. And what about your wife, Lisa.? She made it clear in the press that she wasn't happy with the prenup you made her sign?"

"She had nothing before she met me, and trust me, she wouldn't risk going back there again."

"Okay, well, I've got my work cut out for me."

"You certainly do."

Chapter Three

LOOK AT ALL THOSE BALLS

After the meeting, I headed to the player's locker room to talk to Rickie. Besides the information I already had on each management team member from Redman, I also Googled them. I have to say, Google is fantastic. You can find out things about anybody. I started with Rickie, verified some things, and discovered others. As reported, Rickie was both a star basketball player and academically gifted. He turned down a science scholarship from Harvard to pursue the NBA, was the number one draft choice of the Jacksonville Stars, and got the biggest rookie contract in the league.

But despite all his accolades, it turns out Rickie had a little skeleton lurking in his proverbial closet, and it didn't involve drugs. A couple of years after he signed with the Tigers, a woman filed a paternity suit against him. She said they had a baby together. Rickie denied the accusation and said it was just a scam to get money, but the L.A. press had a field day with it and made it sound like Rickie was guilty. While it was proven Rickie wasn't the father and the woman was just a deranged groupie, the negative press affected his reputation with his fans and the rest of the league, and Rickie was furious. In addition to being humiliated, Rickie gets even angrier when Redman doesn't support him in the press, making it look like he believes the allegation. Could revenge be a motive for blackmail? And would Rickie be trying to get even with Redman? And even though it makes no sense for Rickie to use himself as bait and ruin his career, it's another possibility. And all possibilities have to be considered. My dad would tell me that the person you suspect the least is usually the one who did it. And the more suspicious you are, the greater your chance of finding the truth.

The hallway to the players' locker was filled with pictures of the Tigers' championship games and players. It was a veritable memorial to some of the best athletes and games in Tiger history. As I took out my cell phone and took pictures, I wished my dad was there with me and could have seen it. I realized I should have taken more time to appreciate and enjoy him when I had the chance. Sorry, Dad.

When I got to the players' locker room, an enormous white security guard stopped me as I started to walk in.

"I'm sorry, sir. This entrance is only for the team," he said as he stepped in front of the door.

"I'm Sam Razor, the new head of security."

"Sorry, sir. Nice meeting you. I was told you were starting today," he said as he shook my hand. "My name's Robert, I'm the security manager."

"Nice meeting you, Robert."

Since I never know where leads to solving a case will come from, I make it a point to get to know everyone and make them feel comfortable telling me things. And if there's one group in the company that has helpful information, it's the security department.

"How many security officers do we have?

"Five, including me. We all cover the facility for home games and the locker room, and two of us travel with the team for away games."

"How long have they worked for the company?"

"Three of us are long-term. Ten years, five years, and three years, respectively."

"And the other two?"

"They're new. The old security director hired them before he left."

"Do they all have security experience?"

"Yes, sir. Most of them have worked for other pro teams before they joined. Would you like to meet them all?"

"I would, but not today. We'll have a meeting tomorrow."

"I look forward to it, sir. Here to see anybody in particular?"

"Rickie."

"He's in the gym," he says as he steps from the door. "And welcome aboard again."

"Thank you, Robert."

I walked into the locker room, expecting to find a sweat-stained collection of lockers and benches, but instead, it felt like I walked into the Presidential Suite at the Four Seasons. I knew professional athletes were pampered, but this was pampered plus. The place was carpeted with thick plush carpeting and adorned with expensive designer furniture, positioned in front of big, beautiful mahogany lockers resembling walk-in closets. Seeing how pro athletes were treated made me wish I had become a pro basketball player—all the money and women I would have. There was only one problem: my height, strength, and lack of ability; otherwise, I would have been great.

I walked through the locker room and into the gym. The team led by Johnson was scrimmaging, so I sat on a bleacher seat and watched. In addition to Rickie, the rest of the starters were on the court, and I got to see my favorite players up close. Tommy Washburn was the six-ten forward from Ohio State and the team's second-best player. Washburn was a top player in college and was drafted in the first round, the same year as Rickie. It was reported that Tommy and Rickie didn't like one another. Tommy wanted more money and didn't like that Redman refused to renegotiate his contract until he was done with Rickie. The rest of the team included Mike James, a six-foot-five-point guard from Georgetown; Lucius Allen, the seven-foot center; and Leroy Thompson, the other six-foot-six forward and the oldest player on the team. Leroy was the second-best forward in the league and was retiring after the playoffs. And, like a lot of the other players in the league, he was broke and needed money. He was also angry that Rickie got all the publicity, and he was never mentioned, no matter how well he played. Rickie told the press that Leroy was a crybaby and a mediocre player and couldn't retire soon enough. So, considering all the animosity between the players and Redman, **could one of them be behind the blackmail?**

While all these guys looked huge on TV, in person, it was like a bunch of sequoias broke into the gym and started playing basketball. And they weren't just big and tall; they were super coordinated and able to contort their bodies to make a basket in ways that weren't human. Or at least in ways that weren't human for me. As I watched the scrimmage, Johnson came over and sat beside me.

"What do you think of the team, Sam? he asked.

"I think the championship is in the bag," I replied, smiling.

"Yeah, we'll see. How's your first day on the job going?"

"It's going," I replied.

"Can I ask you a question?" he asked.

"Absolutely."

"How did you meet Phil?"

When I heard the question, my suspicious investigator senses kicked in, and I knew I needed to be careful.

"Through a friend that did some work for him."

"I see. This is a tough job you're undertaking."

"What do you mean?" I asked.

"You got a lot of huge egos, all jockeying for appreciation from Phil," he replied.

"Does that include you?" I asked to get a sense of his honesty.

"Absolutely," he said, standing up and giving me an arrogant look. "But I deserve it," he smiled and walked away as the practice finished and the players entered the locker room.

Yeah, there's something about that guy that I don't like. But that doesn't make him a blackmailer, not yet anyway. Before I returned to the locker room, Jerry Redman walked out onto the court.

"Hi, Sam," he says. "Getting the lay of the land?"

"Yeah. Meeting the organization. What about you?"

"Came to talk to the Coach about some hot prospects for next year's draft. But I'll be back in my office later if you want to talk to me."

"I do. I'll swing by your office."

"Perfect. See you then," he says and walks into the gym.

Remembering that Johnson was on his cell phone this morning, talking about having to handle something, and Jerry was on his phone telling someone everything would work out, could they be partners in the blackmail? My mind raced as I returned to the locker room and found Rickie getting dressed after his shower.

"Hi, Sam," he said. "How's it going?"

"Good. I am just getting to know the organization. That's why I came to see you. You got a second?"

"Sure. Let's go into the coach's office. He's still talking to Jerry," he said as he led me to an office at the back of the locker room, and we sat down.

"Coach Johnson doesn't mind you using his office?" I asked.

"Sure, he does, but I don't give a shit."

"Yeah, I know you two don't get along."

"He's an asshole, but he has to tolerate me, and he hates that," he replied with a smile. "Now, what did you want to talk to me about?"

"Earlier today, when we first met, you mentioned weird things happening."

"That's right."

"What kind of weird things? As head of security, I need to know if something's happening that could affect the organization."

"Let's just say there're been a few strange conversations I've overheard that concerned me."

"Who was involved in those conversations?"

"Jerry Redman and Coach Johnson. I walked in on an argument and heard Johnson say he would quit if things didn't change."

"What do you think he meant by "change"?" I asked.

"It's all over the press that he wants more money, and Phil isn't budging because of me."

"You?" I asked, but I already knew.

"My contract's up, and I'm negotiating with Phil, and Johnson knows it. So, he's been trying to find out what I'm asking for."

"Who's he talking to?"

"I've heard he's talking to Jerry and Christina to find out what they know and to threaten them with quitting if he doesn't get a sizeable extension on his contract."

"Do they know about your negotiations with Phil?"

"I'm sure Christina does. As President, she'd have to, but she wouldn't say anything to Johnson, but Jerry would if he knew. He and Johnson are best buds, and both hate Phil."

"Why?"

"Phil's too smart. He knows neither one means as much to the team as I do, and he won't give them more money until he and I have an agreement."

"Any other weird things?"

"Yeah. There's been a lot of theft lately."

"Theft? What kind of theft?"

"Personal stuff taken out of lockers and never found. Wallets and jewelry."

"Did the old security guy know about this?"

"Yeah, but he couldn't figure it out. All the players think he was the thief," he said and smiled.

"Did you ever have anything stolen?" I asked.

"No. I keep my personal belongings locked up. I also have some extra security."

"You do."

"Yeah, I give the security manager, Robert, extra money to keep an eye on my locker. He's outstanding. You should talk to him."

"I intend to. Is there anything I should know about between you and other players?"

"Pretty cagey, Sam. You know about the problems between me and Thomson?"

"Just what's been written in the press. Has that been blown out of proportion?"

"Most of it. He's a good player but overrated, and Redman knows it and won't give him the contract he thinks he deserves. But the championship is on the line, and we all want to win and get the leverage winning gives you."

"Yeah. Well, thanks for telling me."

"No problem. If I hear anything else, I'll let you know," he said as he finished getting dressed, and I walked out of the locker room.

I had just started walking back to the executive offices to talk to Redman when Lisa Redman walked up. She was dressed in a skin-tight spandex leotard with intentionally positioned peek-a-boo holes that showed off various parts of her gorgeous body, but I knew from our first meeting that I needed to keep my eyes firmly placed on her face.

"Hey, Sam, how's your first day going?"

"Everything is going well. I'm just getting familiar with the organization."

"What about you?" What are you up to?"

"Just getting ready for cheerleading practice."

"I see."

"Well, I've got to go; I'm late already."

"Before you go, can I ask you a question?"

"Sure."

"I heard there have been thefts in the player's locker room. Do you know anything about that?"

"The old security director looked into it when he was here, but I don't think he found anything. Or at least I didn't hear about anything."

"And what about the rumors about there being animosity between the players? Is that true?"

"Of course it is. They might be talented athletes and make a lot of money, but they're just kids. And you know how jealous kids can be."

"Yeah.

"Oh, shit, I'm late," she said as she looked at her watch. "Since we've got our next home game tomorrow night, the cheerleaders are waiting for me in the gym to practice, so I have to go. Toddles," she said and walked away.

As much as I liked watching her walk away, something she said didn't make sense. I just came from the gym and didn't see any cheerleaders. Was she lying to me so I wouldn't be suspicious about why she was there, or did she make a mistake and think the cheerleaders should be there? I decided to follow her and find out. When I got back to the gym, Robert greeted me again.

"Welcome back, boss. Did you forget something?"

Knowing how to lie without creating suspicion is one of the talents you develop as a private investigator, and considering I'd had to do it many times in my career, I was an expert.

"Yeah, I needed to use the bathroom but got sidetracked when I was here before."

"I understand," he said and stepped aside. "Hope everything comes out okay," he said jokingly as I smiled and walked back into the locker room.

Once in the locker room, I ducked into the bathroom and waited a minute to give Lisa time to enter the gym. Then, I exited the bathroom and took a position out of sight at the gym door. No other cheerleaders were in the gym, and Lisa was privately conversing with Leroy Thompson, away from the other players. Lisa was flirtatiously touching his arm as they shared a laugh. Since Leroy was retiring at the end of the playoffs and needed money, and Lisa was already pissed off about the measly amount of money she'd get from Redman if the marriage went south, how they were acting raised my suspicions. Could they be behind the blackmail? At that moment, Johnson started walking to the locker room, so I left before he saw me.

"Have a good day, Robert," I said as I left.

"Yes, sir," he said. "You, too."

On the way back to Redman's office, I thought about what I had learned from my visit and concluded that I still didn't know who the blackmailer was. All I had were more suspects. When I thought about Lisa and Leroy, I was a little jealous. If she was the one planning the blackmail and I could get her to touch me that way, I'd help her myself. Not having a woman's touch, or at least from a woman who didn't hate me, made me a little sad. Since my divorce, the only female companion I'd had was my mother. And even she didn't like me all that much. Redman wasn't in his office when I got back, so I went to my office, shut the door, sat down, took a pad of paper, and started making notes about what I'd learned from my visit to the gym.

First, there was the talk I had with Rickie, and him telling me about Johnson trying to find out about his deal with Redman and that he was expecting to get what he wanted despite Johnson's interference. While I already knew there was no love lost between Rickie and Johnson, I knew Johnson was underhanded enough to do whatever he needed to screw things up for both Rickie and Redman if need be. And that led me to my conversation with Johnson himself. His statements showed me that he was suspicious about who I was and why Redman hired me. He also informed me that every ego in the organization was looking for financial recognition, especially himself. And then there was Jerry Redman. And even though his appearance in the gym to talk to Johnson about supposed new talent seemed innocent enough, I remembered he was talking to someone earlier on his phone and saying things would work out, so maybe he didn't come to the gym to talk about new talent, but the blackmail. And then there was Lisa. Even if nothing suspicious was going on with her, I just liked thinking about her. As I finished making notes, someone knocked on the door and Christina Redman walked into my office.

"Hi, Sam, can I talk to you?" she asked sitting down.

"Hi, Christina. What's up?"

"I heard you spent some time in the gym."

"Yeah. I heard about some thefts in the locker room, so I was checking into it."

"The old security manager looked into it, too, but didn't find anything."

"That's what I was told."

"Can I ask you a question?"

"Sure."

"My father told me you were a successful private investigator before you came to work here. Why did you give it up?"

"As I said, when my friend, Peter, told me that your father was looking for a head of security, I couldn't pass up the opportunity to be a part of my favorite sports team."

"Your friend's name is Peter Walsh, one of our marketing guys. Right?"

"Right."

"How do you know him?"

"I did some investigative work for him."

"What kind of investigative work?"

"I'm not at liberty to say. It's private."

"I see. What ..."

Before she could continue her inquisition, Redman walked into my office.

"Sam, I need to talk to you. Oh, hi, Christina."

"Hi, dad."

"Can you excuse us?"

"Sure."

She got up and started to walk out.

"I'm sure we'll get to talk again, Sam."

"I'm sure we will."

As she left the office, Redman closed the door and sat down.

"What did she want?"

"She was trying to find out why I really came to work here."

"What did you tell her?"

"I told her the truth, that Peter told me you were looking for a new head of security."

"Did she accept that?"

"Probably not. But she's not the only one asking."

"Who else?"

"Couch Johnson. I went to the gym to investigate and spoke to him. He asked about how you and I met. And I told him the same thing."

"I got another note from the blackmailer," he said, taking an envelope out of his pocket and handing it to me.

I opened the envelope and saw the note. It was handwritten and said, "Only five days left."

"When did you get this?"

"I found it underneath my office door this morning."

"This one's handwritten. Do you recognize the handwriting?"

"No."

"I'm assuming you have signed contracts from the management team and the players?"

"Of course."

"If you'll give me copies, I'll compare them to the note."

"I'll give them to you before you leave. Did you find out anything else during your visit to the gym?"

"Nothing concrete. Just things we already knew. Rickie knows Johnson is trying to find out about his contract, and there's animosity between some players and Rickie. And there's been some theft in the player's locker room, but you knew about that already."

"Yeah. We have filed a few insurance claims for things like watches and jewelry but never found out who the thief was."

"Well, if you have nothing else, I need to go home and walk my dog."

"Do you like dogs, Sam?"

"Not really, he was a going away gift from my ex-wife."

"Let me get you the contracts," he said as he left my office.

After I picked up the contract copies from Redman, I went home. Frank met me at the door, letting me know he needed to go out.

"We're going, so hold it for a few more minutes. I don't need you decorating my rug again," I said as I put on his leash and walked him down the block to the park at the end of the block.

As Frank sniffed around for a suitable bathroom, I started thinking about the note and that my time was running out to find the kidnapper. Frank finished his business, and as we began to leave the park, an attractive, dark-haired woman in her thirties walked up to me, holding her Chiwawa.

"Hi, Frank," she said as she set her dog down, and the two dogs started the obligatory smelling of each other's rear ends.

As I watched them, I couldn't help but think that if my ex-wife and I had done more of that while we were married, maybe we'd still be together.

"They seem to know each other," I said.

"Yeah. Maryann and I were friends and would come here every day to walk our dogs.

"You were friends with my ex-wife? Why didn't I ever hear about you?"

"I moved away before she met you. But we still talked, and I heard about you and your divorce. My name is Rebecca Wiles," she said, shaking my hand.

"It's nice meeting you, Rebecca; I'm Sam," I said, returning the handshake.

"Are you and your husband back here for vacation?"

"No, I moved back by myself last week after my divorce was finalized."

Hearing she was unencumbered, I turned on the charm.

"So, you come to the park every day at about this time to walk your dog?"

"Yeah, right after I get home from work."

"What's your dog's name?"

"Sparky. And you and Frank come here every day, too?"

"Oh yeah. It's either here or my living room rug," I said, smiling, and she laughed.

"Well, it looks like Sparky is done, so I should be going," she said. "Maybe I'll see you here again. Bye, Frank."

As she started to walk away, I stopped her.

"Listen, do you like basketball?"

"I love it. The Tigers are my favorite team."

"I work for them."

"I know, Maryann told me."

"Would you like to see tomorrow night's playoff game?"

"That would be wonderful."

"If you give me your phone number, I'll call you tomorrow, and we can arrange a place to meet," I said, taking out my cell phone, and she put her number in.

"Well, then I'll talk to you tomorrow," she said, walking away.

I watched her walk away and then took Frank home. Because I met Rebecca, I was ecstatic to have Frank in my life. That night, in between thinking about Rebecca, I spent the night looking over the signatures on the contacts and comparing them to the note Redman got, but none matched. So, after having a drink, playing with Frank, and thinking about Rebecca again, I went to bed.

Chapter Four

UNABLE TO MAKE THE CALL

On the way to the arena early the following day, I thought about the blackmail note and tried to figure out who wrote it. When I got to the office, Redman was already there.

"Sam, did any of the signatures match the note?"

"No."

"So, what's your next move?"

"I want to interview them all again."

"Are you suspicious about anybody?"

"As far as I can see, the person who stands to benefit the most from accusing Rickie is the coach. If he goes public with the accusation and gets Rickie off the team, he thinks that makes him indispensable to you and forces you to agree to his contract demands, and if he doesn't go public, he gets the seventy-five million from you. So, he wins either way."

"Do you think he's working alone?"

"I don't think so; he couldn't pull it off alone."

"Who else do you think is involved?"

"I'm not sure, but there are a couple of other people with a motive. Your brother and your wife."

"My brother, I can see that, but not Lisa. She's not that vindictive."

"Maybe."

"What's the next step?"

"I'll start with Johnson after tonight's game. And if I can get copies of the insurance claims and theft reports you filed for the locker room thefts, I'll talk to Robert, the security manager about them."

"You think the thefts have something to do with the blackmail?"

"I don't know, but I want to find out."

"No problem. Also, I've arranged for you to watch the game from my box tonight."

"That's great. I'm bringing a date to the game, and sitting in your box will impress her."

"It worked for me with Lisa when we first dated," he said, smiling.

"I'm sure your money didn't hurt either," I laughed.

Before I met with Robert about the thefts, I called Rebecca and arranged for her to meet me at the arena before the game.

"That's right, the team's owner is arranging for us to watch the game from his press box."

"Sam, that is fantastic. I'm so excited. I'll see you tonight."

"See you then," I said, hanging up the call.

Her excitement on the phone turned me on in ways and places I hadn't felt in a long time and made me smile with anticipation. After reading the reports and insurance claims, I went to the locker room to see Robert. He wasn't at the locker room door, but I found him in the gym, watching the players warm up, and I saw Johnson in his office talking to Leroy Thompson. I wanted to wish him luck in the game, so I knocked on his door.

"Come on in," Johnson said, and I walked in.

When I entered the office, the two men stopped talking and looked nervous.

"Hi, Sam," Johnson said. "What can I do for you?"

"I came to wish you and the team good luck tonight."

"Thanks. Is that all you wanted?"

"Yeah," I said and left the office.

As I walked back into the gym to see Robert, I thought about Johnson's and Leroy's nervous reactions when they saw me. They were hiding something, but was it blackmail?

"Hi, sir," Robert said. "Are you looking for me?"

"Yeah, let's go into your office for a minute."

"Yes, sir,"

We went to Robert's office, shut his door, and sat.

"So, what can I do for you, sir?"

"I've reviewed the insurance claims and security reports from the locker room thefts and have some questions.

"Sure."

"According to the reports, all the thefts happened within the last couple of weeks."

"That's right."

"And they were all written by you."

"Yes, sir. Me and the old security director."

"Tell me about the thefts in your own words."

"As the reports said, the things stolen were jewelry, watches, and cash out of players' lockers."

"Who were the players stolen from?"

"Almost all of them except Rickie and Leroy Thompson."

"I heard from Rickie that he's paying you to watch his locker?"

"Yes, sir. I didn't want to take his money, but he insisted. But don't worry; I ensure the security guards watch out for all the players."

"I'm sure you do. Why do you think Leroy hasn't experienced any theft?"

"I don't know. He keeps his locker locked."

"And the rest of the players don't?"

"Not all the time. Even though we tell them to, some of them don't."

"The report says the amount of cash stolen was pretty significant."

"Yes, sir. In total, it's about twenty thousand dollars."

"And you don't have any suspects?"

"No, sir. I interviewed all the players and the maintenance people and didn't find out anything."

"And Thompson was the only player that didn't have anything taken?"

"That's right."

"Okay, thank you. I'll see you tonight at the game."

"Yes, sir."

As I left the office and started to leave the locker room, I saw Johnson come out of his office and watch me go. On the way back to the executive offices, I thought about Johnson and Leroy's reaction to seeing me. Considering Leroy Thompson was the only player who didn't have anything taken but was also the only player who needed money and was going to retire after the playoffs, in my mind, he was the main suspect in the thefts and possibly involved in the blackmailing plot with Johnson.

I met Rebecca at the arena's front entrance an hour before the game that night. She looked fantastic. She was wearing tight-fitting jeans, a low-cut blouse, and high heels, and smelled so good I just wanted to stand close and sniff.

"You look great," I said.

"Thank you, Sam. I can't thank you enough for inviting me to the game."

"It's my pleasure."

We walked into the arena and passed a security guard stationed at the entrance.

"Hi, Mr. Razor, sir. It's nice meeting you," one of them said and shook my hand. "My name is Steven Ross."

"Nice meeting you, Steven. We'll talk tomorrow," I replied.

"I know, sir. That's what Robert said."

"Well, keep your eyes open and be safe."

I said, and Rebecca and I walked to the arena elevators.

"The security guards seem professional," Rebecca said.

"They have to control unruly fans, which can be dangerous."

I took Rebecca up to Redman's box, which was packed with celebrities and dignitaries, and Phil met us at the entrance.

"Hi, Sam."

"Hi, Phil. Please meet my date, Rebecca."

"Nice meeting you, Rebecca," he said, shaking her hand.

"Thank you for inviting me to the game, Mr. Redman."

"Please call me Phil."

"Why don't you find a seat," I told Rebecca. "I want to talk to Phil for a minute.

"Sure, Sam. And good luck tonight, Phil."

"Thank you."

While Rebecca sat down, Phil and I walked into his private office.

"I spent more time in the locker room today and learned some things."

"Tell me."

"Well, first of all, I found Johnson talking to Leroy, and when they saw me, they seemed nervous, like they were talking about something they didn't want me to hear. Then, when I spoke to Robert about the thefts, he told me that in addition to the jewelry, the money stolen from the locker room was nearly twenty thousand dollars, and Leroy was the only player with nothing stolen."

"You think he took the money and is working with Johnson on the blackmail?"

"We know Leroy needs money and is retiring after the playoffs, so Johnson could be using him to help with the blackmail with the promise of getting some of the money."

"We're running out of time. Only four days are left, and the next two games are on the road."

"I know. That means I've got to figure out who's involved by the time the team returns."

"Yeah. And I need to arrange to get the seventy-five million ready, just in case."

I returned to Rebecca as he walked away, and I realized the hundred-thousand-dollar bonus was slipping away. The game was great. The lead changed hands at least a hundred times and was tied in the fourth quarter with thirty seconds left, and Rickie had the ball. The arena crowd went wild with anticipation as he drove to the basket for a layup. A shot even Helen Keller would have made. But he missed the shot. As a devastated hush fell over the crowd, the Blazers got the rebound and scored as the game ended. It took a minute for the crowd to realize the Tigers had lost and leave the arena.

Rebecca and I were both in shock as we walked out of the arena and didn't say anything until we got to the parking lot.

"I had a great time, Sam, even if the Tigers lost," she said.

"Me, too. Where did you park your car?"

"I didn't drive, I took an Uber. I don't deal well with a lot of traffic. I arranged to have them pick me up at the arena entrance after the game."

"Call them and cancel. I'll take you home."

"Are you sure?"

"Absolutely. You're too depressed to be alone," I said, smiling.

"You're right," she said, returning the smile. "And you, too."

I drove her back to her apartment and walked her to her door.

My Dad taught me to be a gentleman and always said, "Even if you're trying to get lucky, be a gentleman and treat a lady like a lady."

And he always treated my mother like a lady all the years they were married.

"Would you like to come in and have a nightcap?" she asked.

"I don't think so. I've got an early game meeting tomorrow morning. But I would like to see you again, besides with Frank at the park."

"I'd like that," she said and kissed me. "Good night."

"Good night."

As I drove home, I thought about the kiss and realized I didn't want Rebecca to be a one-night stand. She was special, and I wanted to get to know her better before we went to bed. Then, we would have many one-night stands.

I woke early the following day to walk Frank, hoping to see Rebecca. But when I got to the park, I saw her with Sparky and another man. While Sparky and Frank gave one another their welcome sniff, Rebecca walked over with the man.

"Hi, Sam," she said.

"Hi," I replied.

"Sam, I want you to meet my ex-husband Paul. Paul, this is my friend Sam Razor."

"Nice meeting you, Sam," he said, shaking my hand.

"Yeah, you too," I replied.

"Paul is here to finalize some details of our divorce."

"And to ask her to take me back," he said, putting his arm around her and smiling.

Hearing that, I decided it was time to excuse myself.

"It was good seeing you, Rebecca, but I've got to get to work. Nice meeting you, Paul."

"You. Too, Sam."

"I'll call you later, Sam," she said as she pulled away from Paul.

"Sure," I said and left the park with Frank.

On the way to the arena, as I thought about Rebecca and Paul, I must admit I felt jealous and sad. If she were still seeing her ex-husband, and he had plans to get back together, any plans I made for her and me wouldn't happen.

"Oh well, I still have Frank until FedEx makes another delivery."

When I go to the arena, I went to Redman's office to talk to him before the meeting, but he was already in the conference room by himself, having coffee and reading the newspaper's sports section.

"Good morning, Sam."

"Good morning. What did the paper say about the last night's game?"

"Take a look," he said as he showed me the headline on the page.

The headline in big, bold letters read, "The Tigers Blow it." The series is tied one to one because of a missed layup by their star player, Rickie Wagner.

"Wow," I said, handing the paper back to Phil.

"And they're right. Rickie hasn't missed a layup like that since he was a baby," he said. "I wonder what happened?"

"Besides missing that shot, he played a great game. He scored thirty-five points."

"Yeah, but we lost, and that was a home game. Now we go on the road, and by the time we come back here, there will be only one day left until the money has to be paid. And since the Blazers have never lost a game on their home court, we could be down three to one when we return here. So, what's your next move?"

"Since everybody will be gone for the away games, I want to come in tonight and check out the player's lockers to see if I can find anything. Can I get keys to the arena?"

"Yeah," he said, taking out a key ring and handing it to me. "It's a key to the back entrance to the arena. The security code and alarm company phone number are also on the key. I'll put your name on their list so you call them when you unlock the door and tell them who you are."

"Got it," I said as I put the key in my pocket."

At that moment, the management team entered the conference room, took seats at the table, and Phil started the meeting.

"It was a tough loss last night," he said. "Anything to say about it, Coach?"

"Rickie screwed up is all I can say. He should have made the shot to win the game, but he didn't."

"But he had a good game besides that," Christina said. "If it weren't for him, we wouldn't have been that close."

"That's right," Jerry Redman said. "So, he missed a shot. He'll make up for it next game."

"He better," Johnson replied. "We have to win at least one game on their court and tie the series before our next home game."

"Yeah," Phil said, "When are you and the team leaving for New York?"

"This afternoon," Johnson replied. "I want to get there and acclimate to the time change before the game."

"Are you taking your plane to the game, Dad?"

"Of course. I'll take you, Lisa, and Jerry with me."

"What about Sam?" Christina asked."

"I'm not going. I've got meetings with the security department about the thefts in the locker room."

"Have you found out anything?" Lisa asked.

"A few things, but nothing concrete. Hopefully, I'll have them solved soon."

"Okay," Phil said. "If there isn't anything else, let's get ready to go to New York and win a couple of games."

After the meeting, Phil, Jerry, Lisa, and Christina left for New York on Phil's plane, and Johnson, the team, and the away security guards left on the team plane. I met with Robert and the remaining security guards and discussed the thefts and what we could do to ensure there wouldn't be anymore. Later that day, I couldn't stop thinking about Rebecca on my way home. I was tempted to call her but decided I didn't want to come between her and her husband if she wasn't interested. Since I would only be home long enough to walk Frank and head back to the arena, I put on his leash and dragged him to the park. He didn't like it because it upset his leisurely bathroom routine. After all, he'd been locked up in the apartment all day and looked forward to going to the park and taking his time. I completely understood. I wouldn't have liked someone forcing me to take a crap, but I didn't have a choice; I was in a hurry. Frank started sniffing around when we got to the park, and as he took a leak, I heard another dog barking frantically. I looked over and saw Rebecca and Sparky walking toward us.

"Hi, Sam," she said as Sparky and Frank commiserated. "How are you?"

"Fine. Are you here with your husband?"

"No, he went back to his home. Sam, I wanted to call you and explain, but I wasn't sure you wanted me to."

"That's funny because I wanted to call you, too, but wasn't sure I should."

"My husband and I aren't getting back together. I don't want to."

"Why not?"

"Because I don't love him anymore. I have another man I want to be with."

"Do I know him?" I said, smiling.

"Very well," she said.

"Is it Frank?" I said, smiling.

"No, it's you," she said and kissed me.

"I'd like to stay and keep kissing, but I've got to work tonight. But how about having dinner with me this Saturday night?"

"Okay, but only if you let me cook. And you have to bring Frank."

"It's a date. We'll see you then," I said, gave her another kiss, took Frank home, and left for the arena.

I couldn't stop smiling on the drive. Concentrating was tough; her kisses were all I could think about. When I got to the arena, I used the key Phil gave me to unlock the back entrance, called the security company, gave them my name, and walked in and headed to the locker room. Besides the security lights throughout the building, I expected the basketball court and locker room to be dark, but as I got closer, I could see all the locker room lights were on, and I heard noises. Being cautious and not knowing what I was walking into, I took out my gun. When I entered the locker room, I saw a white man in his thirties dressed in a janitor's uniform standing in front of an open locker.

"Move away from the locker," I yelled and pointed my gun at him.

"Don't shoot," he said as he shut the locker."

"What are you doing in here?" I asked as I moved closer, keeping my gun aimed at him.

"I'm with the overnight janitorial company."

"Sit down. And keep your hands where I can see them."

He put his hands up and sat on the bench.

"What's your name?"

"Whose asking?"

"Sam Razor, head of security for the team. What were you doing in that locker?"

"Cleaning it. Like I always do. It's part of my job."

"How did you open that locker?"

"Janitorial company gives me a key."

"Is that right? What's your name."

"Ronny Jackson."

"Ronny, we've had a few things stolen from the lockers over the past few weeks. Know anything about that?"

"No."

"Any idea who it could be?"

"No, but there are a lot of us working on this account. If you're done with me, I need to leave. My shift is over," he said nervously.

"As a precaution, before you go, I'd like to check your pockets."

"Why?"

"Just to show me that you're telling me the truth."

"I don't have to do that. You're not the police."

"You're right, so I'll just call the police and have them check," I said as I took out my cell phone.

"No, you don't have to do that."

He empties his pockets on the bench and only has a few coins.

"Satisfied?"

"Yeah, thank you. I want your telephone number and home address if I need to contact you again."

"Okay," he said as I put his contact information in my phone.

"Thank you. Have a good night."

Chapter Five

THE FINAL SECONDS OF THE GAME

On my way home from the arena, I listened to the game on the radio. With five minutes left in the fourth quarter, the Tigers were up by ten points, and Rickie had scored forty for the game. His missed layup in the previous game was in the rear-view mirror, and the Tigers were up two to one in the series. When I got home, I was going to call Phil in New York on his cell phone to tell him about my visit to the locker room and that I thought I had found the locker room thief, but since I couldn't prove it yet, I decided to wait and called Rebecca instead to tell her I was taking Frank to the park.

"You're home from work?" she asked.

"Just got home."

"Did you get everything done you wanted to?"

"I think so. Want to go with me to take Frank to the park?"

"I already took Sparky, and I'm getting ready for bed."

"That's too bad; I looked forward to seeing you."

"Well, when Frank's finished, why don't you come to my place for a nightcap?"

"I'll be there in just a few minutes. I have a feeling Frank will be quick."

I hung up the phone, ran Frank to the park for a quickie, and went to Rebecca's for the rest of the night. I know I said I wanted to take my time and get to know her before we had sex, but after a couple of drinks and some making out, I decided we knew each other well enough, and we made love. And it was fantastic. And even though it had been a long time since I had been with a woman, I thought I did pretty well. I knew all the right body parts and movements and didn't remember sex ever being that good with my ex-wife. But then again, I can't remember anything good about her.

The following morning, Rebecca and I had sex again, and I went home, changed clothes, and left for the arena. She offered to take Frank and Sparky to the park so I could call Phil and give him the news about the thefts. And even though I hadn't found the blackmailer yet, I felt positive I would. When I did, I would use the hundred-grand bonus to take Rebecca on a romantic European vacation and pop the question. No, not about marriage, about her and Sparky moving in with me and Frank.

When I got Phil on the phone, I told him I had some news he had to hear.

"What is it?" he asked. "Is it good news about the blackmail plot?"

"No, it's about the player's locker room thefts. But it's better to give you all the details in person."

"I'll be back in L.A. tomorrow morning and meet you at the office."

"Perfect," I said. "Good luck tonight."

The following day, after another exciting night with Rebecca, Phil walked into my office and sat down.

"I saw we lost last night's game," I said.

"Yeah, now the series is tied two to two and coming back to L.A. tomorrow night for game five. But forget that. I got another note this morning," he said as he took another note from the blackmailer out of his pocket. "It says the money is due tomorrow before the game and I haven't been able to secure the funds. If the blackmailer goes public with the accusation before the game, I'll have to pull Rickie."

"We still have time."

"Yeah. Tell me about what you found out about the thefts.

"Last night, when I was looking around the player's locker room for information, I met a night janitor checking out the lockers. I'm sure he's the one who's been stealing things."

I knew I wasn't telling him I'd found the blackmailer, but I thought he'd still be happy. But he wasn't. He looked confused."

"This guy works for the janitorial service?" he asked.

"Yeah. That's what he said."

"Sam, we don't have a night janitorial service."

"You don't?"

"No, what was the guy's name?"

"Ronny Jackson."

"Ronny Jackson. Wait a minute. I'll be right back," he said, leaving my office and returning with a folder. "This is Johnson's personnel folder," he said as he looked at the paperwork inside. "And here is an article in the newspaper about a relative of Johnson's named Ronny Jackson, being convicted for theft."

"You're kidding. So, he lied to me. I need to find him and find out how he got into the locker room."

"Did you get his contact info?"

"Yeah. I had him give me cell phone number and home address."

"Call him and have him come in so we can talk to him."

I took my cell phone and dialed the telephone number he gave me.

"Nobody's answering. I'll go check out the address he gave me and see if I can find him."

"Be careful."

On the way to the address I got, I was pissed at myself for making the rookie mistake of believing him about being with the janitorial service. I don't make mistakes like that. But now I knew he was connected to Johnson and could also be connected to the blackmail plot. The house was in a poor section of L.A. with a lot of drug addicts. I drove up the street looking at the address and found the one he gave me. To be as inconspicuous as possible, I went further up the street, parked, and returned to the house on foot. The house looked dark, but the drapes in the living room were open. As I was about to look in, I saw a car approaching the house, so I hid behind a tree and watched. The car, a Mercedes SUV with 'Main Man' plates I knew belonged to Johnson, parked in front of the house, and Johnson and Ronny got out of the vehicle and entered the house. I took out my cell phone camera and took a picture of them together so Johnson couldn't refute that they knew one another. I waited for another photo of them leaving the house, but Johnson exited the house by himself a few minutes later, returned to the car, and drove away.

Knowing Ronny was a convicted felon, I figured he owned a gun and wouldn't be afraid to use it and that he probably had the stuff he stole out of the lockers in the house. But to find it, I'd need to get a search warrant. So, I called my brother. Marco was a detective for the L.A. police department, and we would occasionally collaborate on cases. I would call him when I needed background checks on potential clients, and he would call me to get information on one of my past clients that he was investigating. Private Investigators and the police department didn't get along. Cops feel that investigators get in the way and steal their thunder, and investigators think the police are incompetent. I told Marco about Ronny and that I felt I had probable cause to think he had valuables he stole from the Tiger players in the house. He agreed to get the search warrant and meet me.

An hour later, Marco and another policeman showed up with the warrant, and I knocked on the door.

"Ronny, it's Sam Razor and the police, open the door."

A moment later, the front door opened, Ronny appeared, and Marco handed him the search warrant.

"What the fuck is going on?" Ronny said, looking at the warrant.

"I know you lied to me about being a janitor, and I know you stole things from the Tiger players," I said. "So, we're here to see if you have any of it here."

"That's right," Marco said as we entered the house. "So, sit down and don't interfere."

Ronny sat, and the other policeman stood next to him.

"This is bullshit. You don't have any proof that I took anything."

"Not yet," I said.

We searched the bedroom, opened every drawer, the closet, and under the bed, and found nothing.

"I know it's here," I said, seeing a large jewelry box on top of a dresser. "He wouldn't be trying to hide the jewelry and watches he took. He didn't think he'd ever be caught," I said as I opened the jewelry box and found at least fifteen costly watches, gold chains, and cash.

"Bingo," Marco said.

"Yeah," I said, taking the jewelry box into the living room and showing it to Ronny.

"Where did you get this stuff?"

"I bought them," he stammered.

"And the cash?"

"I cashed my paycheck today."

"No, you stole all this stuff, and when I prove it, you'll go back to jail for a long time."

When he heard jail, he knew he was caught ,and his demeanor changed.

"Listen, can we make a deal?" he asked.

"What kind of a deal?" I asked.

"I have information about coach Johnson, that I know you want, but I won't tell you unless you agree that I can return everything I took and get a reduced sentence. And I'll only give the information to you, Sam."

"Okay," I said.

"We'll be right outside the front door if you need us," Marco said, leaving the house.

"So, tell me," I said to Ronny.

"Do we have a deal?" he asked.

"That's going to depend on what you know."

"Coach Johnson is my cousin, and when I got out of prison, he contacted me about helping him and making myself a lot of money. He said he was in the process of negotiating his new contract with Redman and he was asking for a big raise. But he also knew Redman was negotiating a huge new contract with Rickie, which meant no money wouldn't be left to pay him. So, he devised a plan to blackmail Redman using Rickie as bait. He knew that Redman wouldn't risk losing Rickie and the championship and would come up with a lot of money to keep the phony drug allegation about Rickie from going public."

"Did he know you were stealing from the players?"

"No. He gave me a key to the arena, got me the janitor's uniform, and had me put the blackmail notes where Redman would find them. That way, he wasn't involved. The stealing part was all me."

"I need you to come with me to the arena and tell your story to Mr. Redman. And we'll talk about your deal."

"Let's go," he said.

Marco cuffed Ronny and took him and the stolen goods to police headquarters for booking. I drove back to the arena and tried to find Phil to give him the update, but he was gone, and so was the rest of the team. So, I decided to go home, see Rebecca, and walk Frank and Sparky. I started feeling better about catching Johnson, stopping the blackmail, and getting my bonus, so when I saw Rebecca, I hugged and kissed her.

"What are you so happy about?" she said, returning the kiss.

"I'm close to solving a big case that has a big payday for me," I said, smiling.

"Oh, Sam, that's fantastic. Is it something you've been working on with the Tigers?"

"Yes, but I can't say any more until it happens."

"Understood. How about letting me take you out to have a pre-celebration dinner?"

"Sounds good. But I need to walk Frank first."

"I already took Sparky to the park, but we'll walk along with you and Frank."

"Let's go."

After I walked Frank and he played with Sparky, Rebecca and I went to dinner at one of my favorite restaurants. A former client, Luigi Rodrigues, owned it and was the only Italian/Mexican restaurant in L.A. The menu was an eclectic mix of Italian/Mexican dishes, like Chicken Alfredo tacos and Angel-hair burritos.

"This is so interesting," Rebecca said. "Where did you meet Luigi?"

"He hired me to prove his wife Maria was having an affair with his head chef."

"Did you prove it?"

"Yeah. I had to pretend to be a busboy in the restaurant for a week and finally caught the chef and Maria in the back room one night, making more than new menu items."

"Why can't you tell me more about the big case you're working on?"

"It's not finished yet, and I have to keep it to myself until it is."

She tried several more times to get me to tell her, but I kept it to myself. My dad would tell me that a detective's loose lips could sink a case. And the more we kissed, the more I could feel my lips getting looser. After dinner, we returned to my place with the dogs and spent the night. We took the bed, and Frank and Sparky slept on the floor.

The next day, I met with Phil and updated him on what Ronny told me.

"You believe him?" he asked me. "He's a liar and a crook."

"I agree, but we don't have a choice. The jewelry and cash he had were stolen, which I verified with the insurance claims, but he wants us to agree to support a lesser theft charge before he confronts Johnson. And since the deadline for Johnson to go to the press with the accusation about Rickie is today, we have to believe him, so he'll confront Johnson."

"I don't want anyone else in the organization besides Christina to know about what's happening. Let's bring Ronny, Johnson, and the police to my house and confront Johnson there."

"How will you get Johnson to come?"

"I'll tell him I want to talk to him about his contract. Bring Ronny to my house in a couple of hours so I have time to arrange the meeting with Johnson. Here's the address," he said as he wrote it down on paper.

"I'll let my brother know and meet them at the jail to get Ronny," I said as I stood up to leave.

"Sam, before you go, I want to say thank you for finding out about Johnson, stopping the blackmail, and saving Rickie and the championship."

"You were the one who knew Rickie was innocent from the beginning."

"But you were the one that proved it."

"It was a team effort," I said, smiling.

I called my brother, told him to bring Ronny to Redman's, and gave him the address.

On the way to Redman's house, I couldn't stop smiling. While I got lucky in finding Ronny in the locker room, I did pretty good work getting him to confess to the robberies, rat out the coach, and stop a seventy-five-million-dollar blackmail plot. And that's how the meeting went. Accused by Ronny face to face, Johnson admitted he planned the blackmail to force Phil to give him the money he thought he deserved. Since the plot didn't work, instead of filing charges against Johnson, Phil fired him and told him he would let what he attempted be known by all the teams in the NBA so no other team would hire him and offered the Tigers head coaching job to his brother Jerry. Because of Ronny's cooperation, Phil agreed to let him return the stolen jewelry and cash, dropped the felony theft charges, and charged him with only petty theft. A misdemeanor that carried only a year's sentence and three years' probation. He gave me my hundred-grand bonus, a box at the arena, and offered me a full-time position as Director of Security for the team. I decided I would rather watch Tiger games, so I declined.

The next time I saw Phil and the management team was at my wedding. That's right, I asked Rebecca to marry me, and for some strange reason, she said yes. We held the wedding at Phil's mansion in Beverly Hills, where Frank and Sparky acted as the ring bearers. They were cute, but getting them to walk down the aisle with the rings took forever. They kept stopping and sniffing one another. After the ceremony, Rebecca and I went to Europe for our honeymoon, and while we were there, I read that Rickie and Phil had finished their contract negotiations, and Rickie was now a part owner of the team. But what happened to Rebecca and me while we were on our honeymoon almost cost us our lives, but you'll have to read my next case to find out about it.

THE END